White Tree

Sonia Edwards is from Cemaes, Ynys Môn. A previous winner of the ACW Book of the Year Award and the National Eisteddfod Prose Medal, she is an acclaimed poet and fiction writer. She now lives and works in Llangefni, Ynys Môn.

White Tree

Sonia Edwards

PARTHIAN

Parthian
The Old Surgery
Napier Street
Cardigan
SA43 1ED

www.parthianbooks.co.uk

First published in 2001
by Gwasg Gwynedd as *Y Goeden Wen*
Translation © Sonia Edwards
This edition: 2006
All Rights Reserved

ISBN 1-902638-51-4
   9 781902 638515

Cover design and typesetting by Lucy Llewellyn
Cover image: Mihangel Arfor Jones
Printed and bound by Dinefwr Press, Llandybïe
Editor: Gwen Davies

Published with the financial support of the Welsh Books Council
and Llenyddiaeth Cymru Dramor / Welsh Literature Abroad.
www.llen-cymru-dramor.org / www.welsh-lit-abroad.org

British Library Cataloguing in Publication Data

A cataloguing record for this book is available from the British
Library.

And all night long we have not stirred,
And yet God has not said a word.
Robert Browning

And Daybreak said, with frost on its breath:

What did it feel like, Nen? Being unfaithful? Having another man come inside you after all those years of being married? You were almost like a virgin, weren't you? Almost pure.

I sensed all your fears. After that first time. After you'd burrowed beneath each other's skin and your scents had become one. After he'd had to go because the dawn was breaking and the two of you were a secret like the moon itself. And then the old melancholy came, didn't it, and gripped you, sweet Nen. It purred deep inside you, smugly claiming you back. It churned up your longing and taunted you with memories – a faraway childhood that would never return but the smell of it still new like clean white towels

1

dried in sun and fresh breezes.

You longed for him, Nen. Longed for your handsome lover as he drove away, the headlights of his car piercing the dusk: piercing, disappearing. Yes, dear Nen, you pined – for your lost virginity, perhaps. For little-girl-springtimes when life was simpler and men were unapproachable strangers with deep voices disturbing the purity of things.

When you were an innocent child, sweet Elen.

But you're a sinner now. A pretty one, mind you. All sweetness and light.

You are, you know, Elen. Sweet Elen. You too can remember the night.

MEDI

There were two men in love with her.

'There are two men in love with you, Nen.' Envy spiked my words.

Nen looked at me for a long time. She'd sensed its taint and I knew I should have kept quiet. We'd been best friends since school. Inseparable, me and Nen. Shared things.

'But I only love one of them,' she said softly. Oh, so softly. Like whispering to her own soul. Whispering to someone who already knew her secret.

And I knew who it was. She'd confided in me from the start. She was brimming over with it. Almost boasting. Bursting to tell. And I felt almost ill when she did. I saw her bloom during this new love affair. She grew. Owain had kindled something in her. I said to her soon after: 'You're sparkling, Nen. What's he doing to you?'

She liked to say his name. She said his name then, rolled it off her tongue with a pretty little sigh. I imagined her breathing his name when they made love, when he was pleasing her, stroking her, his fingers on her, in her....

Oh, fair-haired little Elen, you didn't know, did you? How difficult it was for me. Being your friend. Yes, it was a good feeling. In the beginning. A warm-summer-feeling. You and I only three years old and forever in front of us, constantly changing colour, fresh as our cotton dresses. I was the eldest. And you were mine. You were my friend and I looked after you better than a sister would have done. It was no trouble though! That was what I wanted. You needed me, but I needed you too, needed the secure feeling it gave me to hold your delicate little hand tightly in mine.

'You don't approve, do you?'

But it wasn't that, was it? I wanted you for myself, didn't I, Nen? Coveted you. And you knew nothing. No-one knew. About the jealousy fraying my insides as I lost you intermittently to a host of boyfriends. Well, you always were a pretty little thing. Sweet with it. It was easy to see how you were able to make them fall for you. And you did your share of falling in love too. They turned your head. Even broke your heart. But I was there for you when things fell apart, drying your tears and trying silently to hold my own heart together, knowing I could never have you. I could only be there for you, to hold you as friends do, to drop sisterly kisses into your hair....

'No, Nen, it's not that I don't approve....'

4

Her look pierced me sometimes, somehow reaching the very marrow of my bones where the truth lay, naked and white like her flesh when she offered her body to him....

'I'm a bad girl! I know that....'

Her mischievousness made her look even prettier. Grains of it floated upon the angst in her eyes. Eyes that had learned to dance because of him. I'd warned her as she first became besotted with him, 'Don't sparkle too much in front of them, Nen. That's the first sign, believe me....'

Of a woman having an affair. Oh, the thrill. The arrogant escape to fuck someone in secret. Returning with her secret warm and damp between her thighs. And that's all it was meant to be. An escape. A bit of fun. She told me that. Confided in me. Right from the start. When she began to 'sparkle'. Told me everything. We were best friends. What else are friends for? Then things changed. The sparkling became something bigger, more dangerous. And that's why I hardly turned a hair when she said: 'This is bigger than I thought, Medi. Bigger than I'd ever thought love could be. It's taken me over now.'

She was wringing her hands. Her eyes wandered. She seemed frightened of her own restlessness. So this was what it was like. This soppy joke that existed in novels, in black-and-white films when yesterdays were a cheap fantasy. This love thing. But here was someone in love for real and it wasn't pretty. Nen wasn't free to love Owain. Owain wasn't free to love Nen. But they both wanted each other until it hurt. So she said. I didn't want to believe her. And yet I knew in my heart that I'd never seen anyone in real life look the way Nen did when she said how much she loved him. There was something sacred in her confession. Pure, even. Something almost absurdly chaste and perfect and pure in this reckless girl who was deceiving her husband, deceiving another man's wife, endangering the security of her own children. Oh, Nen. You wouldn't have had to have gone through all this pain if you'd turned to me.

'Say something, Medi.'

She wanted me to fill the void, the distance that had grown between us since she said that she loved him. So much. I hated the force of her feelings towards him. It didn't make sense to me. And it wasn't as if he even knew her properly. Not like I knew her. Since forever. Since when everything was morning fresh. Since when she was unable to pronounce her own name at three years old. Couldn't say 'Elen'. Only 'Nen'. Nen. Same word as 'heaven'. And as we grew older I wanted so many times to clear the clouds from her eyes. So that she'd look, and see me properly.

'What do you want me to say, Nen?'

'I don't know. Something friendly. Say you understand.'

And how I wanted to say that I did. But it wasn't the same kind of pain, was it? A vein of sunlight swelled through the grey. A grey day. Just ragged bits of cloud and that spittle of rain freckling the faces of things now and again. Until now. Now a gobbet of sunshine seemed to want to make up for things and Nen was saying, before I could answer her, 'I used to hate selfish people.' The words tore through her breath like an old pair of scissors.

It was then that I got to hold her. She smelt clean and sweet like flowers in a warm room. I breathed in her smell as a mother would her child's; filled my senses with her sweetness, and the tang of her tears was like the taste of salted butter in a biscuit.

She didn't move. The swell of her breasts was soft and even beneath that skimpy T-shirt, little apples of breasts.... Hush, Nen, I'm here for you... salty and sweet and the veil of her hair over both our faces.

Nen shivered suddenly. A little tremor. It quivered there – then nothing. Two nerves wincing like the touch of wings. Maybe she was cold. The sky had soaked back the sun. Cold. Yes, maybe. Even though I held her tightly. Too tightly, until her trembling fingers plucked at my own nerves. Oh, Nen, I wanted to tell you then that I understood. Understood what had awakened you.

She sat motionless as a rag doll, doing nothing, not resisting, only bending to my movements as if she had no choice. Her compliance gave me a strange kind of power over her, and awakened within me beautiful, awkward feelings that I couldn't ignore.

She let me kiss her. When I finally opened my eyes she was looking at me unquestioningly like an intelligent sheep-dog obeying a bizarre command. She hadn't judged me. She'd used me, maybe, to do her own penance. All she said was, 'I did know, Medi. I've known for a long while. How you feel.'

I knew then that I could never love anyone as I loved her. But that would have to be from a distance from now on. I'd lost her to my own greedy kiss.

She put on her cardigan awkwardly. There was charm in her little-girl movements – the way she smoothed creases, rolled up her sleeves, the way she looked down instinctively, involuntarily searching for lost buttons before going home as if she were still a nervous child. Watching Nen get herself ready to go was like watching a rabbit grooming itself. It was an endearing ritual, a series of sudden but graceful movements: that touching up of hair and lipstick just in case, before rummaging in her handbag for car keys. The whole process was part of that incredible ability of hers to compose herself in a hurry and face things.

We stood there then. At arm's length. Our words didn't touch either. I didn't ask her when I'd see her again. Only said, 'You couldn't be selfish if you tried, Nen.'

But her watery half-smile only suggested that she didn't believe me.

It was after Nen had left that the rain came. Large pustules of rain. Instead of staying in neat droplets they spoiled the window-pane with their splattering.

Selfish rain. Taking without offering anything in return.

And the Day sang its own worried song:

It's late afternoon. Night will soon fall. My light will grow dim till there's no light at all.... Who's to blame? Who's to call?

Tick-tock, tick-tock.... A clock. Tick-tock.

A sound. It's a world full of sounds. Shrill. A harassed, five o'clock world.

Tick. Tock. Five. Says the clock.

Where are you, then? Where?

Here.

Somewhere.

Hiding beneath all the sounds. Roaring, snoring, fizzing, hissing. Hiss-hiss-hissing. Almost kissing, wet tyres on tar. Hiss-ing, hiss, hiss, kissy-kiss kissing, the quick-step breathing of frantic lovers muffled beneath the long day's frazzled covers.

Where did you go? If you didn't go home. Will you go – come – back home? Too soon to worry... get into a state... just because it's late....

'My pretty maid, come back to me, for I will sing a song for thee....'

But there's no rocking chair by the fire. No lovesick shepherd on his lonely mountainside. No orphaned lambs... no children pining. Yet.

Hiss-hiss. Kiss-kiss. Tick-tock goes the clock.

It won't be five o' clock for ever.

Before too long it'll be too late.

And where will you be, Nen? Who'll be to blame then, when the stars in the sky have bled themselves dry?

Who will know why?

Tick-tock. Tick-tock.

A clock.

PUW

'She walked out, Sir.'

He was one of the more sensible ones. Used to looking after Number One. Streetwise as they come. And for once his eyes seemed to synchronise with his gob. Hadn't taken anything, obviously. Well, not yet.

'What d'you mean "walked out", Smiler?' I wasn't going to call him by his proper name just because there were two coppers sat there with us, was I? Neither he nor I – nor his own mother, come to that – could bloody remember what it was by now, anyway.

'Just went, didn't she, Sir. Took her handbag with her.'

What the hell did that prove? Any teacher with half a brain would have taken her bag with her when she left the room – even if it was only to go for a pee. You wouldn't leave your handbag with a classroom full of thieves and druggies like this lot. Bloody vandals. And I'm the one defending them in meetings with other head teachers about pupils' welfare. The disadvantaged. Begging for more funding so that we can offer them 'broader opportunities'. Them and their fucking headlice. But this lot were there when Elen Rees went. They were there creating mayhem. Being deliberately disruptive. Making a shitty day ten times worse. And then I thought: Christ! Maybe this mad bugger was one of the last ones to see their teacher alive. It left me cold. His upper lip was covered in sores.

'Were you misbehaving, Smiler?' Bloody stupid question. Like asking if the Pope preferred kissing tarmac to kissing women.

Smiler looked at me with something like pity in his eyes. The little bastard. I turned to the constable. He was young, too. Fancied himself. His face wore a scissor-like expression laced with acne.

'They're a difficult class,' I said. 'You need the patience of Job with them.'

Smiler squared his shoulders and the constable's face clouded: who the hell was Job? I felt that familiar irregular flutter in my chest. It needed guts. Just to walk out. Wish I'd had the balls to have done that a long time ago. Before this place started killing me slowly, day after day, choking me with my own tie.

'Is there anyone your staff can confide in – that is, if they're stressed out?'

A reasonable question, Mr Detective Inspector. The

young policeman tried to look intelligent. A good move, usually. I remembered that Smiler was still standing there.

'Right, then,' I said to him. 'You can go.'

He stared dully. 'Where to?' his sheep's eyes asked. 'To Hell if you like!' replied my own. He turned on his heel. Abuse, my arse. A good smack would do the little shit the world of good.

Then I told them we had Wil.

'Who?' The detective perspired. He'd forgotten his own question, his face taking on the hue of boiled lobster. Bet your blood pressure's right up there too, mate, I thought.

'Wil Adamson,' I said, 'Senior Teacher. People usually go and see him.'

About filling in forms for travelling expenses and input about teacher training courses. We dreamed up a fancy title for him three years ago, before the HMIs arrived. Everybody got a written job description then, even the plastic penis Jonsey used in the Sex Education lessons. That was big enough for a mule, that was, and some smartarse had drawn a face on it in permanent ink. Anyway, by the time we had the Inspection, we too, like every up-and-coming school, had our own Professional Tutor.

'Bloody nonsense!' Wil had said. Didn't stop him holding out his hand for a pay-rise, though, or complaining about having to sacrifice a weekend of golfing and boozing for an induction course to enlighten him after his meteoric rise into Middle Management. But none of us would have dreamed of asking him for personal advice, would we, and that's a fact. Not with his own life in such a mess. A bottle of whisky? Probably. Phone the Samaritans? Maybe – if

15

push came to shove. Ask Wil? No bloody way, José! That would have been Pure Desperation. Like having a death wish. Dealing with somebody else's sexual/financial worries would have pushed him over the edge, what with the stress he's under.

'Can't sleep nights, Puw,' he keeps saying to me. 'Can't cope.' Can't get it up either, according to Jonsey. Been four months like that. Well, he would confide something like that in Jonsey, wouldn't he, because he's got all the text books on that stuff. Mind you, Wil's wife's a right bitch. And that's half his problem, if you ask me. They say the snotty cow's getting it somewhere else. Must be blind, whoever he is, because she's an ugly bugger. But Wil's alright. An OK bloke, deep down. It's this job that's made him boring. He could do with a good woman to ink a permanent smile on his dick, too.

'Perhaps we'd better have a word with Mr Adamson, Sir?' The young constable again. Keen. Looking at his boss as the latter looked at his watch. And me knowing that they might as well save themselves the trouble. Knowing Wil would freak when he heard that two coppers wanted him. I went to look for him myself, leaving Starsky and Hutch with two floating teabags and a packet of Penguins.

'Who?' said Wil.

'Elen Rees,' I said.

'The blonde one? Didn't she go home ill?'

'She didn't go home. Full stop.'

'What?'

'Just went. Walked out. No sign of her. Nobody's seen her since yesterday morning.'

'What – just disappeared? Just like that?'

'Apparently she'd been acting a bit strange. Quiet. Distant. That's what the kids in the class said.'

'Jesus! She walked out and left a class?'

'Smiler's lot,' I said, as if that justified a teacher legging it. And judging by the way Wil's eyebrows hit his fringe, it probably did.

'What do the cops want with me then?'

'You're the Professional Tutor, right? The staffroom's answer to Claire Rayner. They thought she might have confided in someone like you if something was worrying her.'

Wil's eyebrows remained in his fringe. And before he could start on me with his, You daft bastard, why didn't you tell them she'd never confide in me routine, I stuck my oar in first.

'Got to let them conduct their enquiries. Go through the motions. And let's face it, it's part of your bloody job, this. Staff welfare.'

Wil stubbed out his fag. Hitched up his trousers. Picked his nose with his thumbnail.

'Newpapers'll love this,' he said. 'TEACHER CRACKS UNDER PRESSURE OF UNRULY CLASS. I can just see it now. They'll be lapping it up. Teachers flipping because of the kids in this place. They'll have a bloody field day!'

I hadn't had a chance to think of that. But that's Wil for you. Your typical tabloid reader. In the end the cops interviewed all the staff. Some of the sixth formers too. A strange kind of hush kept coming over the place – even though the noise never actually stopped completely. But there was less of a buzz in everybody's conversations. Something that happened in news bulletins was actually happening here, drawing them, drawing all of us into this mystery, this strangeness that was beginning to form its lingering mass over everything, like a chemical cloud.

I'd never given very much thought to Elen Rees. Never really had much cause for doing so. She was quite a popular teacher. Quite competent, too, to be fair. Never caused a fuss about anything. Husband. Couple of kids. Drove a Mondeo. Just your regular teacher, really. Not the type to just disappear without a word to anyone. I thought about Loopy. Half-hippie, half-crazy. An eccentric artist-turned-teacher, whose Art lessons were a psychedelic mix of slap-happy paintbrushes and debates on legalising cannabis. Now if Loopy had legged it one morning and disappeared faster than a line of coke on a mirror, nobody would have thought very much of it. But it wasn't Loopy who went, was it? He was still there with us, saucers for eyes that shone brighter than usual. Poor Elen, he said. Disappearing, just like that!

No, there was no stereotype, was there? No hard and fast rule. No bloody sense in it at all.

Smiler was one of the first ones into the yard when the last bell rang. Scrawny shoulders, that woolly Umbro hat pulled down low over his forehead. His whole attitude was already a kind of warning: look at me – would-be burglar. Or worse. The trainers on his feet were the most expensive kind. But his belly was empty, his brain emptier still, and his repertoir of swear words beat hands-down even Wil Adamson on a Friday night. He stopped brazenly just outside the school gate and hunched his shoulders to light a cigarette. I did exactly the same. Filled my mind with smoke. Smiler jovially raised two fingers at one of the school-bus drivers before he disappeared.

It's strange, watching someone until they disappear completely from view. Until they get smaller and smaller and then they're nothing. Like Smiler did. But he just disappeared out of view. Round the corner.

There was no doubt at all that Smiler would return.

And the Voice came, shrouded, as if through a veil:

You hadn't kissed.

For a long, long while.

No touch of lips.

No smile.

I saw.

I saw you. You drew the veil, Sweet Elen. Drew the veil over yesterday because its light hurt your eyes. And you tried so hard to shut out its arrogance: get thee behind me! You are a

Past wearing horns that tear through my guilt.

Was it your conscience, Nen, begging to prevail? So you drew down the veil?

But it slipped back, didn't it, like a draught under a door?

Yesterday can be like that.

Lithe as a cat.

It kept returning, again and again.

Yesterday came back for you, Nen.

GARI

It was a fling. Nothing more. No big deal. But Elen got her money's worth out of it, didn't she? Wouldn't let me forget it. Kept harping on. Picking at the scabs of a marriage still bleeding.

Liz was sexy in the way a men's magazine is sexy. Sexy in a wonderfully common way. Obvious – sexy in that way a woman wearing clothes too young for her can get away with if she's got the legs for it. And fair do's, she did have great legs. Not such a fantastic bum, though, and her tits were nearly too big for those skimpy tops to look perfect on her, but Hell! The whole package was good. Did things to a bloke. And the long, bleached hair made me forget the laughter lines around her eyes.

It was never a question of being in love with Liz. Never a problem. She wasn't – it wasn't – love. She was only a fuck. And an average one at that. No earthmoving tremors. There was a lot of insecurity under the peroxide and that throaty laugh. Looking back I suppose I was a bit of a bastard towards Liz too. I never thought someone like that could be so vulnerable. In an odd way she was more fragile than Elen was. Easier to wound inside because she didn't wear her feelings on the outside. I was never able to see how much I was hurting her too.

I remember telling her that Elen knew about her in the same way that someone can recall an item in a news bulletin: just feeling distanced from the whole thing. She answered with a simple: 'Is it worth it, then? Getting up to go home?' In the lamplight she looked almost pretty. But her voice held no gentleness, only a flat practicality. The bed smelt of sex. 'I know you'll never love me, Gari.'

Her sudden perception shook me up a little as I realised that she'd never expected anything from me. Her breasts looked longer and whiter and more blue-veined than ever before. I turned my back on her as I got dressed. She lay on her side, making no effort to conceal her nakedness; the slackness of her belly marring the line of her body. Lying there now, nothing mattered any more. I wanted to draw the duvet up and around her, to be kind. But she was right. She could hang on to her dignity because she chose to be shameless. 'I'll see you, then.'

'Yes.'

So false. So fake. That sad cliché for pretending not to say goodbye. And those words stood for too long between us, like the after-taste of stale wine. I went home without having a wash, and it was almost as if I could smell her loneliness on me too.

It was Elen that I had on my mind as I drove home. The old Elen with the sun in her hair. I thought things would come right. When she saw I meant it. That everything was over between me and Liz.

When I walked in she smiled at me. A 'Hi, love, had a good day?' kind of smile. Offered me a cup of tea, even. Couldn't quite understand why she seemed so relaxed. She didn't even know I'd just finished with Liz. Poor bloody Liz. My clothes still smelt of her.

'Elen, listen – I... we've got to talk.'

'Talk?' There was something alien in the way she said it. A kind of disbelief. Talk? As if I'd just suggested hitting her.

'Yes, talk. About us. You and me.'

'And Liz?'

'What?'

'I take it that Liz is part of all this too?' As if she were hellbent on pushing our names back together.

'I don't understand?'

'You and Liz. You want to be together. That's what you wanted to tell me, isn't it?' She spoke slowly, as if she were explaining something to a simpleton. 'I understand. And I'm OK with it. You go to her.' And she smiled. 'Go on. It's all right.'

She hadn't been drinking. Her voice was too steady. Too logical. She wasn't even being sarcastic.

'It's over, Elen. Liz and me,' I waited for her expression

to lighten. Soften a bit. 'I don't want Liz. I want... you.'

She frowned ever so slightly.

'I'm not trying to get back at you, Gari.'

'What?'

'I just don't love you any more.' She said it so quietly and with a horrible finality. That should have been my line and I didn't need it now. I only needed Elen but it wasn't her any more.

'You haven't wanted to touch me for ages,' she said, 'and now I don't even want you to.' She was almost apologetic now. 'That doesn't... you don't hurt me any more, you see. I don't care now. I'm not bothered what you get up to with anybody.'

She poured the tea. Set it down in front of me like a kindly aunt.

'I don't want to leave, Elen.' I hated myself for not being able to keep the panic out of my voice.

She shrugged her shoulders. A nonchalant gesture. Her voice was almost gentle.

'Please yourself.'

I drank because the words refused to come. Because there were no words. The tea was too hot, scalding my insides, but on the outside I was cold, freezing cold in the face of this confidence of hers. Elen, my wife, was out of my reach like a woman in a photo. But how could I blame her for acting like this? I wanted to, though. Jesus! Wanted to bang my fist on the table till the cups rattled. Wanted to tell her to take a look at herself, at the way she'd cooled towards me during these last months, turning her back on me in the night. I wanted to raise my voice, but I didn't have one.

26

'I'll sleep in the back room,' she said. When I tried to look into her eyes, she added, 'I've already moved my stuff there.'

It was as if my own story was being rewritten, as if all the familiar things around me – the furniture, the curtains, everything, even the walls of my own home – belonged to somebody else. I looked for revenge in her voice but there was nothing but indifference. She even sounded kind, which was worse. A tinge of jealousy, hatred even, would have made me feel better. But she held all the cards because she felt nothing. She'd won hands down. And the irony of it was that she hadn't intended any of it.

'Night, then, Gari.'

I just wanted to touch her, shake her, make her feel something. I wanted to force myself upon her: come here, you cold bitch, because I'm your husband and you do what I say. But I didn't. Jesus, no. I just loved her and didn't know how to tell her and now I knew I was losing her and there was bugger-all I could do. I felt like some poor penniless sod watching his last fire go out.

So this is what it feels like. Being rejected by someone you really love. So this is the emptiness, the sheer panic of it? Is this what hurt is – your life shuddering slowly before your eyes like a jerky slide show? Click, click and around they go: too-white faces, sand and sun, old folk and kids and birthday candles. Photos of kissing ghosts caught by the sun.

Photos of Elen.

With golden hair.

I should have kissed you more often when the sun was upon us.

And the dark-mirrored Depths called out from beneath the bridge's furrowed brow:

You came, then?

Was it just to look down? I'm still here. Do you want to come to me?

What does it feel like now, Nen? The black water beckoning and then....

Shh! Can you hear?

The water beneath you, coming, sighing... ah! Such sweet death as nightfall catches every breath.

29

Are you coming
to bed with me?

To let the water set you free?

Sleep with me, Nen?

SAL

I have good days. Days when I can cope. I take fewer tablets
then. Even get them to wheel in the television set. They're
good to me, bless them. They do what they can. And it's nice
when the sun gets round to this window in the afternoon.
Nice to have a hot, strong cup of tea and feel the injection
starting to take effect. Warms my veins, it does. Daren't take
too much at a time, they say. It could go straight to my head!
As if I were some junkie in a shop doorway! Mind you, I
don't think I'd mind by now if it had that effect. A 'trip'
somewhere might be quite a nice feeling. Weightless. Being
carried on a breeze somewhere where it's bright. No pain.
But it's only on bad days that I get to thinking about that.
About flying. Up and away. About death. On days like this

31

one I dare to think differently. Push death away for a bit longer. I just want to try and hold on for a bit longer when it's like this. It's a thin line between down here and up there. Nobody in their right mind wants to die.

'Look, I'll draw this curtain for you, Sarah. Otherwise you won't be able to see the telly with all this sun!'

'No! Let it in, love.'

She's a lovely little nurse, this one. Understands. And it's more than just the training they get. It's instinctive, the way she gets through to people.

'OK!' She smiles. Shrugs her shoulders and gives me a quirky little wink. She's full of these funny little words. OK. Mega. Super-duper. She cheers me up. And she's chatting again: 'Eisteddfod's on! Just your thing. Highlights from Somewhere-Or-Other!'

It's not everybody's cup of tea, she's right there. Not any more, anyway. She flits away again, giving me a bit of peace, but not before pushing this cursed remote control gadget into my hand. And it is a curse. Can't get the hang of it because I keep pressing two buttons at a time. Still, I won't be needing to change channels for a bit.

They're so bonny, these kiddies. Reciting and singing like little angels. It's a relief to see that even the old-fashioned things still hold their appeal. I like to listen. And remember. Shame they didn't have it on the telly when I used to take the little one to compete.

Thought the world of her, I did, my little golden-haired Elen.

'Don't pause on that word again,' I'd say. 'Look, you're doing it again! Carry it through to the next line.'

Recitation came naturally to her. And she was easy to teach. Didn't sulk if I spoke sharply when she got it wrong. Which she seldom did. And she looked angelic on stage too. We did a fair bit of the eisteddfod circuit. What would she have been then? Eight? Nine, maybe. She won a good few prizes, a lot of them firsts. People loved her. My little angel. 'Yes,' I'd say, 'this is our Elen. My brother's daughter.' So proud of her, I was. As if she were my own child. That's how much I loved her. She spent a lot of her time with me. She was one of four children and didn't get too much attention at home. Not that I blame Ceinwen, mind. She had her work cut out with all of them, what with her sewing and everything. And I loved having Elen. She'd stay overnight often. And we'd have a whale of a time, midnight feasts of chocolate biscuits and the like! The house seemed to wake up when she was in it. Such a little scrap filling such a big place. Such an empty place.... She filled a void deep inside me.

Losing a child makes everything hurt. Inside. And I don't just mean the pain down there, the stuff you feel and see – and have to clean up. It's not just all the blood... and that. It's like mourning someone that you never really knew. Never even saw, except in your mind. Maybe. It's weird. A part of you, gone for ever. Something that was there inside you and you knew it was there without ever needing anyone else to confirm it. Something that had begun to like being there and had decided to grow, like a seed in a warm place. But it's not like losing an arm or a leg or an eye and people saying 'How awful!' because they could imagine how difficult it would be trying to cope

33

without something like that.

Mind you, they did sympathise. In the beginning. Said what was right at the time because it was expected. It was the civilised thing to do. So sisterly and concerned on the face of it, those coffee-morning gossips. She'll get over it, they said. She's young enough. She can try again. Not that difficult, making a baby. Didn't it happen to dozens of women in the first three months? Miscarrying wasn't unique. No use dwelling on it. After all, it was nature's way.

Nature's way has always puzzled me. Everyone for himself. Survival of the fittest. I wasn't one of the tough ones, yet nature would target me, time and time again.

'I can't take any more, Huw.'

The kitchen was full of early evening sun, shadows coming inside to die like the last flies of summer. He didn't lift his head from his newspaper, but he heard me all right. Only pretended not to.

He shook the paper sharply and carried on reading. The remains of that day were so beautiful, clinging bravely to the window pane. I'd miscarried four times. Mourned four times. I remember looking at him. At his pathetic contentedness. At the way he always filled the armchair. *His* chair. The self-satisfied man of the house. Yes, I remember looking at him. Staring, even. Long and hard. He was just slumped there in his stockinged feet. The day was dying slowly, and the simple beauty of it just passed him by. He didn't see it. He didn't see my pain either. It wasn't as if he was aware of anything apart from the usual disappointment. And the mess. But someone else always got rid of that. Tidied up so that he could go back there. So that he could take his pleasure again as if he were burrowing deep into his favourite armchair: Come on, now, Sali. We both need it, see... a bit of loving... we'll help each other through this – yes, like this – now turn over... that's right, do it like that....

I closed my heart to him. Bit by bit. Body and soul. I couldn't bear to have him touch me.

This is all because of last night. All this raking over yesterday's heartache. Last night, when Elen came.

'Mrs Parry – your tablet, dear.'

Time for the next one already. The little white pill. I'd forgotten about it. A treat I allow myself sometimes when the pain seems to forget about me too for a bit.

'You were catnapping now, weren't you? I said this sun would get in your eyes!'

But that's what old memories do to you. You need to be alone, to close your eyes tightly so that you can see their colours. The nurse has turned the volume down on the television so that the voices seem far away, the sound of the children.

'You used to be a teacher, too, didn't you, Mrs Parry – Sarah?'

I'm glad that she chose to call me by my first name. It's the little things like this that I yearn for. They draw people closer and that's what I need as I begin to panic... to slowly count the months as they slip by but refusing to admit it, even to myself. Refusing to admit that it feels as though I'm clinging on to a cliff face, feeling the earth in wet clumps beneath my fingernails, and I'm losing my grip.

'Everyone calls me Sal.' I want to get even closer to her, to the youthfulness in her, the life that's brimming out of her.

'Sal it is, then!' The sound of her voice brings me back with a jolt, snapping me out of my thoughts. Then she asks, 'Sal, where's the bottle of Tamoxifen?' That little brown bottle full of magic pills that are meant to stall the monster lurking inside me. They let me keep them in the bedside drawer.

'Have you moved them?'

No, I don't remember doing that. And yet – I don't know.... We turn the drawer upside down but to no avail. So she has to go and get a fresh prescription. I tell a white lie, that there were only a couple of pills left anyway. That seems to make it less of a tragedy. But the bottle had been almost full. And nobody had been near it. Nobody had rummaged in the drawer. Apart from Elen, that is. When she came last night. She wanted us to look at old photographs together. It was so lovely. She brought me flowers, a bottle of sparkling apple juice.

It was only my golden-haired Elen who'd been looking inside the drawer. Elen. Why, for heaven's sake, would Elen want to steal a bottle of tablets?

She's back now, the nurse. Short of breath yet still smiling. I want to cheer her up.

'You can get off soon.'

She twinkles then. 'I've got a date tonight!'

Putting on perfume. Lipstick. That prickle of excitement. It's like releasing lavender-scented memories from a drawer. You never get too old to remember.

'Lucky you. Is he good-looking?'

36

Her shy blush lights up her face, making her prettier than any make-up ever could.

'Yes, Sal. He's gorgeous!' And that's when she really seems to see me properly. Sees that I understand, that I want to get excited for her too. So that I can remember how it was, how I used to be, slim and attractive. So that I can remember Tommy.

I ask her to wheel the television out of the room as she leaves. The familiar space between the door and the window returns. That white wall where the night shadows congregate like bats. The nights are the worst. Especially in here. You can't get up in the middle of the night to make a cup of tea when you're in here, or leave the back door open so that you can breathe in the stillness and watch the dawn hatch out of the dark.

No, you can't do those things in here.

And the fragile June Sun said:

I came to you. Warmed your back as your mind spun. Nowhere to run to, was there, Nen? Only here, where the kids from the town come with their bikes because it's safer than the street. This was the prettiest place you could find. Early evening. A flirty summer sun. Trees, wooden benches, clumps of flowering weeds. You sat there for a long time, letting me warm you, stroke you...

This is where the river comes every day. A river with rubbish in it, slipping dark as an eel past the backs of the factories where the bad smell is. And I could hear it too, the bleat of the lambs from the nearby abattoir mixed with the smell of blood; you closed your eyes and let me envelop your senses instead. We both heard the birdsong. They were pretending too. The birds. Theirs was a stoic lyricism in honour of me, my sweet reminder that it was nearly summer, even in this apology of a place where the ants wove their way into the warmth and made the gravel path shimmer. And the tinny chimes of the ice-cream van carried fragments of summer from the far end of town: cheap fairground tunes that made you think of music-boxes. Ten-a-penny lullabies and the little ballerina spinning....

Like your mind.

Are you strong?

Or are you weakening?

Every vow you made at the point of breaking....

You couldn't go on. Couldn't mend.

It had to end.

So you asked her. Felt so cold. Inside. No choice.
  You had to go.

Didn't you, Nen?

You had to know.

LIZ

There was lipstick on the sheets. Sheets on the floor. The bedroom was a mess, as if it belonged to a wilful little girl who'd been dressing up in her mother's clothes. Everything was strewn about, the remnants of our playacting – the black stockings shed like snakeskins, and those stilettos he always asked me to wear gleaming boldly amidst the clutter like long-nosed beetles.

We never discussed the future. Our future. It wasn't part of the plan. This thing between Gari and me was just a convenient arrangement. And wasn't I the uncomplicated one? There for him. Always available. A quick-fix fuck where he could live out his fantasies behind closed doors and then go home to the familiar smell of supper and the sound of his kids playing. It didn't hurt anybody. Because it didn't mean anything, did it? Or that's what Gari would say often enough. So often that I began to believe it. Why let feelings complicate things? They got in the way. Messed things up. No. This way we could keep it simple. His words. And I agreed, because I needed to feel the hard heat of his body next to my skin more than I was ready to admit. I needed to feel his weight. Arms. Legs. His wetness, in me, on me, making me a part of him if only for a little while. And when he came, I'd cry out too, getting it right to please him. He liked that. They all do. Compliments them on their manhood. And he never had to know that I was faking it. Pleasuring him came first. So that I could keep him there. Hold on to the warmth of him for a bit longer. And longer. And so it went on.

I would have liked to have felt something too. Something more than his movements inside me. It was as if the hysterectomy had taken all feeling with it. Womb plucked out like the eye from a potato. So neat and clean. Left an emptiness. A convenient emptiness where Gari was concerned. For me, though, it felt like the end of the world.

It wasn't quite that when Gari left me. The end of the world, I mean. He'd never really been mine, had he? Well, not his heart, anyway. I wasn't even sure by then whether I wanted it anyway. I could be selfish again. Liz thinking of Liz. I could ignore my untidy house. Forget to buy wine. I wouldn't have to tart myself up for the sake of a couple of hours when he'd be the only one to see it. I could drink gin in my comfy old slippers and stop having to shave between my legs.

Her voice seemed so steady over the phone. So unexpected. Elen's voice. Almost pleasant. She wanted us to meet. She sounded more formal than formidable, almost as if she were selling double-glazing. Smooth and practised. 'Hi. This is Elen speaking...'

We went for coffee. Giuseppe's in the high street. A Welsh-speaking Giuseppe, pretending, ironically, to be English. A fake Giuseppe with hairs growing out of his nose, wearing a bobbly cardigan.

And it was a shitty cup of coffee as well. Lukewarm. Too much milk.

'Just wanted you to know, Liz. I won't stand in your way.'

'What?'

'Make things difficult, I mean. For you and Gari. You can have him.'

As if she were offering me the remains of a meal she'd had her fill of. Come on. Eat it. I've had more than enough. But she wasn't being sarcastic, or out for revenge. I could have understood that. She was the one who'd been cheated on. She'd already unnerved me by paying for my coffee, smiling, making an effort. I shouldn't have come here. Nobody had forced me to. And yet....

'I've told him too. That I understand. Especially if you love each other....'

'We don't!' My self-esteem was in bits but she wasn't to know that. She fixed her eyes onto mine.

'Are you saying too that this affair meant nothing?'

I couldn't answer. Broken bits of words stuck in my throat. How could I say, Yes, it meant nothing because Gari didn't want me in the way I wanted him. How could I say,

43

Yes, it meant nothing because you can't press a button and make someone love you back. So I said nothing. Sat and watched a skin forming on the surface of the milky coffee.

'A fling, he said,' Elen said. 'Just a meaningless fling.'

My silence must have confirmed all her doubts.

'And to think I went through all this just so that you two could have a fling!' She spat the last word as if it were a bad taste.

There was no-one else in that dingy cafe, apart from Giuseppe reading his paper and pretending that he wasn't listening. Some cheap Italian tenor crooned plaintively in the background, sounding as if his voice was being squeezed out of a tin. All so fake, almost macabre, chewing into the stillness like a serrated knife. Elen looked at me accusingly.

'It's alright for you,' she said. 'You and Gari. People like you seem to be able to walk away from things.'

I wanted to defend myself. To say, no, to shout out: it wasn't me. It was Gari who went. Gari who walked away.... But I didn't, did I? I was the experienced one. Familiar with the night, the smell of gin in the dark. The emptiness. It gave me an odd kind of dignity and I held on to it even though it hurt, felt dirty, like soil under my fingernails. And even though I refused to meet her gaze I knew she was looking at me when she said: 'Feelings are such cruel things. They're stronger than you, they swamp you, take over – when you love someone....'

I knew that she wasn't hurting me intentionally. And that it wasn't Gari she was talking about. It wasn't her love for her errant husband that had brought her that day to that tacky dive of a cafe. But there was someone. He was there, in her eyes, bringing tears to mine. And what she'd just asked me charged the air between us with tension: take my husband away from me, release me, so that I can love someone properly. I could have dealt with it all better if she'd been bold and aggressive. But this wasn't aggression. Or fearlessness. Her eyes were wide open. Great pools of eyes. You could have drowned in them.

She got up suddenly, scraping her chair against the tiled floor, a sound that clashed with the grating tin tenor. It made me painfully aware of my own silence.

'Sorry,' she said. Unexpected. Unnecessary. 'It was a crazy idea, anyway.'

It would have been funny if it hadn't also been so unbearably sad. For both of us. The madness of all this.

Of her apologising to me.

As the cassette player spewed the warbling tenor's heartbreak.

What did he know?

Giuseppe turned to the pages of his newspaper until he found the topless pin-up, and drooled.

And the desperate Messages lit up the screen:

```
         MAIL
FROM: 0889842650

Longing for you!
For tomorrow! xxx
       xxx
```

```
   SENT MESSAGE
     Me too!
    Love you!
     xxx 0
```

```
        MAIL
FROM: 0889842650
Hurry home, darling!
        xxx
```

```
      SENT MESSAGE
    Back tomorrow, Nen.
   You're my everything
        xxx O
```

```
         MAIL
      NEW MESSAGE
      READ NOW?
        [YES]
```

```
FROM: 0889842650

Get in touch. Where are
you? Love love love you
```

VIV

Cessna Citation. Twin engine. Twin propellor. Carried six at most and rocked like a basket in the slightest sneeze of a wind. They'd never have got me in her, Ireland or not. I'd have rowed a boat over to the bloody place before I'd have flown in that. But I needn't have worried. Ow got the Ireland job, didn't he? I remember saying to him that very morning: 'You'd never get me in one of those, mate!'

He laughed and made a few 'you'd shit your pants' gestures. The bugger knew full well that I couldn't stand heights. That was his thing, though, paragliding and all that stuff. Bungee jumps for charity events. All so's he could bloody show off! Hey, look at me! Our Ow's motto, that was. So a boneshaking flight in a Cessna from Llandwrog to

Galway was no big deal for him, was it?

'Go on, then, and I hope you get caught in a Force Ten gale, you bloody Action Man!' I said.

He turned to me with a brotherly 'up yours' gesture before striding over to the car. That's the last time I spoke to him before he set off for Ireland in that shitty little plane. A shitty little plane in a shitty little accident. It never even got off the ground properly. A pathetic, unheroic accident. He'd have been better off killed in a car crash.

I felt nothing when they told me. Their words had no effect, like cold water on a greasy pan.

'Never even got to Ireland, then?' I said lamely. They indulged me in my brainless questions because I was his mate. I knew him. Him and Mari. And the kids. Jesus, the kids. Alun and Ffion left fatherless and there I was, sitting like a zombie in a blue haze of my own cigarette smoke.

It was me who went to tell her.

I'd have preferred to have gone on my own. It was a job that needed doing, and I had to be the one to do it. Rules were rules, though. Even among friends. So I took Christine with me. A true blue policewoman. Born to it. Big feet. Small tits. Practical and totally sexless. Even in black stockings. Nevertheless, she was a good girl. Knew when to keep her mouth shut, keep the bullshit to a minimum. It was almost like having a bloke with me.

Mari knew straightaway. From the minute she opened the door and saw us standing there. It sobers you up, seeing coppers on your doorstep. Even when one of them's a personal friend. Especially when one of them's a personal friend. It seemed as if a shadow's round thumbprint came

50

over her face. Cooking smells wafted from the house, smells of a meal being prepared for someone who'd never come home. A meal for the kids. There was no escaping it. That bloody smell of cooking. Wholesome, homely. Mari was a great cook too. I remembered all the dinner parties, the welcome. Owain and Mari. Me and Siw. Until things got worse between the two of them, the rows. And yet....

'What happened then?' Flat-voiced. No tears. Mari being the way she was. Coping.

'The Cessna... it never took off... nobody's quite sure.'

I tried, clumsily, to explain what I didn't understand myself: just being here in his home made it worse, with the smell of the home cooking he'd never get to taste all around us.

'Cup of tea, Viv?' As if the policewoman wasn't there at all. But Christine took the hint, fair play to her. Her cue to go to the kitchen and find the kettle. One of the unwritten clauses in her job description. Finding tea-making facilities in the homes of the bereaved. Soon there was the clatter of crockery, the clinking of spoons, the hiccupping breaths of a boiling kettle. Good old dependable Chris, lulling us with sounds of domesticity.

'When are you going to let yourself cry, Mari love?'

She looked at me as if the truth were taboo, a deadly disease. I felt like the doctor who knew what was wrong but the pills to cure it had run out. I'd nothing to offer her. The silence became Mari's voice: a voice that had already mourned and cried for a love lost a long time ago.

'Do you know who she is then, Viv?'

'Who?'

51

'The blonde he'd been fucking.'

But she said it so simply, levelly, that it sounded almost lyrical. Grief kept me from blushing. From the shame of having rummaged through his briefcase, destroying the incriminating evidence, the text messages still in the memory of his mobile phone, her photo.... Her. The girlfriend of whom I knew hardly anything. Only that she existed. That she lived in his thoughts night and day. That she meant more to him than any other woman had ever done. That's probably why he talked so little about her. His secrecy protected her and betrayed his own deepest feelings.

'Maybe you can meet her one day,' he'd said once. It was a kind of joke. He was going to end up with her. I could see that in his eyes, in the way he kept her inside himself.

But I know now, don't I, Ow? Know who she is. Was. Know that it was her. I knew straight away. When I saw that photo of her for the second time. The official snapshot now. The blonde teacher. The missing woman. I know a hell of a lot about her now, don't I? That her name was Elen. That you'd given her your heart, your past, your present. She would have been your future too. Even though my own heart wanted to bleed again over Mari, your need for each other shone out of those loving messages winking at me from the screen of your mobile phone. And I felt like a traitor. Because of Mari and the kids. I felt a traitor for protecting you, you cheating bastard. But we were mates, weren't we, Owain? Sharing a desk, sharing fags, sharing the filth of this fucking thankless job as we sat in cars at two in the morning

52

freezing our bollocks off.

Mates. Look out for each other, don't they? To the end. I didn't grass you up, mate, but Jesus, to be honest about it, that was more for Mari's sake than yours. You never knew how much she meant to me. Sweet, faithful, dark-eyed Mari, at home waiting for you through thick and thin. She never knew how I felt either. At least, I don't think she did. Never knew how my insides turned upside down when I looked at her. Thinking about her has often kept me awake till the small hours. And even while I made love to Siw, while I was inside her, taking her, I shut my eyes tightly and conjured Mari into my arms. It all meant something then and Siw would be motionless beneath me, silent, wishing I'd just whisper her name. Was it like that for Mari too? Someone else's name stuck in your throat and you'd climax with a fantasy, coming between the thighs of the woman in your mind? It wasn't Mari who reached you, was it? I was glad, somehow, when I realised that. It was the only way I could steal a piece of her for myself. Faithful, foolish Mari, refusing to break the rules.

Not like that wet June morning. Broke every rule, that did. June without sun, grey and rebellious, refusing to conform. A dirty June. A wet runway. A fuel tank exploding. A basket of a plane, woven with blood.

You'd only just phoned me. You spent your life on that bloody phone. I'd started to think that was what had scrambled your brain. But it was being in love that did that to you, wasn't it? DI Owain Wynne, tough guy, black belt, top bloody bungee jumper. Not so tough though, were you, Ow, when you fell for your pretty golden-haired Elen? Do

53

you remember us that night when we sat in a dark lay-by after that tip-off we'd had? Johnny Cash on the car radio. We listened to whatever came on just to keep awake. And this bloody song was playing. 'What is This Thing Called Love?'. 'Yes,' you said, half-dreamily, unexpectedly, from within your haze of fag smoke. 'Fucks you up, Viv, mate. Brings the toughest blokes to their knees, see.' And that's when I realised I'd never seen you smile from inside like that before.

'Who is she then, Viv?'

And when Mari asked me that, that's all I knew. I didn't know her name then, and yet I knew that she meant everything to you, Ow. And I was so confused. Christ, I wanted to keep your secret, of course I did; wanted to protect Mari too, but in a strange way I kept thinking as well about the golden-haired girl who loved you. Who'd tell her, then? Who sent her that final message?

I'll never forget it. I'd just deleted them. All the text messages on your mobile. Deleted the damning evidence. Held that emptying screen in my hand. And then, suddenly, those bleeps started. Jesus Christ! My stomach turned over. NEW MESSAGE: READ NOW?

Hell, Owain! What was I supposed to do? Just switch it off? Ignore her? How could I? How could I close my ears to the urgent little sounds...

```
    PHONE ME.
   WHERE ARE YOU?
 LOVE LOVE LOVE YOU
```

[ERASE?]

[YES]

[MESSAGE DELETED]

[NO MESSAGES]

And bowing their heads heavy with dew the Flowers said:

We knew

    knew

        knew

           you would come.

You came, Nen.

Before we died.

Became dust.

You knew you must.

We were so fragile as night fell and you came with your grief. Stroked us, each and every one, buried your fingertips in our cold petals,

and the teardrop moon

joined in with our mourning,

encircling your pain

like a wedding ring.

MARI

She didn't come to the funeral. Well, she couldn't have been expected to come, could she? She had no right, anyway. I was his wife. He was my husband when he died. Legally mine. And that kept everything neat and tidy. He was mine so the grief was mine too. I was the one entitled to wear the blackest of black. But even then, I felt I was being cheated on. Even while the earth swallowed him. The jaws of the grave. The wet soil licking its lips.

I half-expected her to appear suddenly out of nowhere, like some tragic heroine, transparent with grief. But even though she never did, she was there, more of a ghost even than Owain himself. I could do nothing except stand there as they all waited for me to perform. Expecting the obvious. The usual show of crocodile tears, pearly ones that bowl the cheek without even smearing the mascara. That's what they wanted. My public display of mourning.

And then – oh, dear God! Somebody handed me a flower. My fingers became as numb as my senses. That moment seemed to destroy me. There I was, in front of everyone, devastated by a single flower. It's only lovers who make a show of throwing flowers onto the coffin. Lovers in books where grief is beautiful.

And so I stood there, the stem moist between my fingers. Stood and stared. I was a shell. The empty shell of the rejected widow. The bastard. He took that last scrap of dignity away from me too. Because it was me they were looking at. Why hasn't she fainted, sobbed her eyes out? That's how it should be. A widow's grief. Why won't she cry? I was the cold fish, my widow's weeds hanging off me almost without touching. Damn him! Even on the day of his funeral he insisted on having the last laugh. Taking me for a fool while I put a brave face on things. As usual. As ever.

I had new shoes. Funeral shoes. Black patent leather, new and unyielding, rubbing relentlessly against my flesh. So I plunged my toes further, deeper into their vice. Then I could feel the new leather searing my skin like a burning wire. And that brought the tears to my eyes. Forced me to bite my lip till it bled. You didn't get the better of me after all, Owain darling. Didn't have it all your own way. An eye for an eye, a tear for a tear.

That's when I felt Viv's eyes burrowing into my thoughts. I was afraid to meet his gaze, afraid of what I might see in his eyes, so I looked down at my feet silently screaming in their painful shoes. Viv's in love with me. Has been for years. Poor Viv. Always so considerate. So kind. Feelings hid clumsily beneath a platonic cover. Thinking I didn't know. And I didn't let on. Till then. Till that day.

It was a sudden decision. To meet his eyes. So easy. I had no passion to offer him, but that didn't seem to matter. Knowing that he stood silently desiring me was enough. Imagining how he'd comfort me stoked a restless warmth between my thighs which spread over me, making me glow shamelessly.

When the last of the mourners had left the house that afternoon, I took Viv to bed. Mine and Owain's bed. It gave me a perverse thrill to realise that the pillow maybe still smelt of Owain. But I was in control. I led him on. It was easy with Viv. Easier. Dear, modest Viv. Viv who was crazy about me. He was obedient, obliging. He'd waited a long time for me. I was adventurous, more daring than I'd ever been with Owain. I took over. Became a whore in my own bed with the flowery sheets that matched the curtains. I could be myself now.

Viv's pleasure was hot beneath my hands – lips touching nipples touching cheeks touching thighs. And it was my name he spoke throughout our lovemaking: Mari, oh, Mari... like a bedside ballad. And I wanted to hear it. To hear my name from his lips. And I tried. Oh, how I tried. But I couldn't hear. Because there were voices... other voices, interrupting, drowning the sound of my name.

The voices of ghosts.

Owain's voice as if through a veil.

Gentle.

Beautiful.

'I love you, Nen.'

And the circling, shimmering Moths said:

Not being able to cry is worse. It imprisons you. Doesn't it, Nen? When the tears dry up. Then you just claw at your own flesh – your thighs, your arms. Tear at your hair until it's a sweaty, tangled mess. But it doesn't hurt, does it? You don't feel your own fingernails, knifelike, furrowing the palms of your hands. You don't see the scratches you've made. Because the real hurt's inside. Inside where the ache is, where there are shards of glass,

there are red-hot coals... dreams curling up like burning scrolls.

Yes, Nen, he was everything to you, all you ever dreamed of in a man. And now your everything's nothing, and your future means nothing more than the ugly bits of wet paper tissues you've scattered where you sit, rocking to and fro like a mad old crone with an empty face.

Then the numbness hits you. Falls over your face like the night. And the skin beneath your eyes pulls tighter, tighter, your cheekbones ache. And you remember – remember the night and its mute voices and the magic all dampened and dead like stars in the rain.

But we can see you, Nen. Behind the swollen mask of your face. We draw near, to where the light came from when he touched you.

We see where the happiness used to be.

And turn our wings into kisses.

SAL

I was shy. I'd never been with anyone except Huw. His way
was the only way I knew. Yes, I was the shy one, whilst
Tommy was experienced, and knew how to please a woman.
And yet that first time his hands trembled too. It was so
beautiful – that little nervousness. It showed that he cared.

'No,' he said, 'don't take them off.'

I'd never worn stockings before while making love. It
had never occurred to me. It was lovely. Whorelike and
lovely. Nylons whispering along his skin. Like a cat licking.
Tiny nails scratching... it was all so different – exciting,
frighteningly new: Tommy wanting me, tasting me, unlock-
ing me with his tongue and our need for each other being
so intense. Oh, it was passionate, beautiful, filling me to

the brim. It won't let go of you. It takes over. That feeling of loving someone so completely. It possesses you, grows inside you and claims your mind like grief. And I did love Tommy. Loved him so much. Loved to love him. Tommy with his come-to-play eyes. Funny. Gentle. Loving.

Married.

Her name was Deliah. A striking name for such a mousey little creature. Her face was always as pale as milk. She had a nervous disposition, a weak chest. Her hair was drawn severely from her face, giving her a martyred look. I'd torture myself thinking about Tommy in bed with her. Imagining his broad, naked back, the rhythm of his body, and her waxen skin beneath him, spent, like a used candle melting into him. It pleased me to think that she was nothing to him but a physical release. It was her duty to let him moan into her, and knowing that made me feel less jealous. But it was me he came to because she wasn't enough.

He was going to leave her. Leave Deliah. I'd leave Huw. Moody, indifferent Huw whose faults made my guilt easier to bear. And within a very short time the guilt disappeared. Being with Tommy reduced it to nothing. It hurts even now; it's there at the back of my mind, rekindling without any prompting. It's the little things that bring it all back – this young nurse chattering about her new boyfriend, things on TV, songs on the radio, Elen. Yes, Elen the other evening, her eyes wandering.... Elen asking about old times.

'Tell me again about Tommy, Auntie Sal.' Even though she knew the whole story. And I remember telling her about the first time: that afternoon of sunshine, pools of light trapped within the net curtains. She was a teenage

Elen then, having just broken up with her first love. Her tears drew my own story from me. A beautiful, tragic love story. I recall her staring at me in surprise, admiration almost. She saw that I understood her hurt and her eyes drew me closer.

'He had a funny name,' she said.

'What – Tommy?'

'No, his surname.'

I told him that too, once. Teased him. Said a name like Tommy Sparrow suited a loveable rogue like him.

'He wasn't a Welshman, then?'

'Next best thing,' I said.

'What do you mean?'

'He was an evacuee during the war. Came to stay with the family at Hendre when he was seven years old. From London. He never went back.'

'Why, Auntie Sal?'

'His mother died... in an air raid – the Germans bombed their street.'

Elen's eyes widened as if she were watching a film. It was a relief after all those years, being able to tell someone. Being able to remember without being ashamed.

'He was a Cockney, then!'

'I suppose so!'

'But he spoke Welsh, didn't he?'

'Oh, yes. Always.' Made love to me in Welsh too. I wanted to close my eyes for a minute, just so that I could remember it more clearly.

'Are you alright, Auntie Sal?'

'Yes, dear....'

'Cry if you want to.'

And I did want to, thinking at the same time how mature she was then to allow me that luxury.

'They all found out about us in the end – our affair was the talk of the neighbourhood.'

'And Uncle Huw?'

'He knew, of course. Knew everything, he and his family. His mother called me a whore....'

Words that were imprinted on my mind. Still are to this day. But I wasn't a whore. I was in love. I still am. I always will be. Loved his memory more than I could ever have loved another living person. Tommy was dead and I was living a nightmare, hunched in a knot of bedclothes all night, waiting for daylight, and when it came, only wanting the night back, so I could conjure dreams of Tommy back with me again. I want want want you, Tommy....

And when Elen arrived at the hospital, hands shaking, it was like seeing myself in a mottled mirror. Like seeing ghosts, a motorbike accident, smoke.

'His name was Owain, Auntie Sal.' Not Tommy. Owain. This was now.

It was as though she were afraid to lay her head on my breast in case she hurt me. My fragility frightened her.

'You're the only one who can understand.'

Her hair was fragrant and soft. Hair that had given him pleasure... and I knew that, deep inside, she was in bits.

'I'm lost,' she said, without seeming to move her lips.

'You loved him, Nen,' I said, and her shoulders trembled beneath my touch as the pet name of her childhood brought

68

back both our pasts.

She remained motionless in my arms for a long time. Feeling her weight warm against me made me feel strong. I was her comfort, whilst drawing my own strength from her. It drew us close. I felt lightheaded – wanted to lift her in my arms, way up high where the air was pure and there were curling clouds. I wanted to take us both from this place, from the sounds of sensible shoes squeaking on shiny floors. Then she said, suddenly, 'I can't fight this pain any longer. I just let it come, let it hurt and hurt until it's burnt out. Becomes a numbness. Until the next time. That's what I do, Auntie Sal. Give in to the hurting until I feel nothing... for a little while.'

I was the one who was dying. Burning up. I was the one with cancer. But these were her words. The words of a woman in the throes of death.

'Will she have a cup of tea?'

My talkative little nurse. Unknowingly, chirpily, she trampled over those delicate moments. Reminded me that I was the one who was ill by adding, a little too enthusiastically to sound convincing, 'Things aren't that bad – your aunt's a real trouper! Had quite a run of good days now, haven't you, Sal? Now, there's no need to get upset, for goodness' sake! We'll look after her.'

She'd missed the point. Couldn't know anything, could she? She had a love life out of a glossy magazine which fitted neatly in between shifts. She knew nothing about hiding behind the mask of her own face, kneading her pain into a wet handkerchief. She hadn't the slightest idea, had she? And yet, what did it matter? Even if she'd known the whole story she wouldn't have been able to offer anything other than a cup of tea, would she? A cuppa, a smile, a thank-you-God that it wasn't her life.

That's the last time I saw Nen. And that's the tragedy of it. Because that's the way I'll remember her now. Thin and pale and tearful. Elen without the gold in her hair. I'll remember the nurse, and the tea that was too sweet. I'll remember those yesterdays, like wounds opening. Comforting her. Failing her.

I'll remember the wet patch where she wept into my nightie.

Remember thinking that there are worse things than dying.

And I'll remember how I drew the curtains around my bed so that I could weep without being seen. So that I wouldn't have to drink tea afterwards.

And the plump full Moon said:

D'you remember that night with its soul shining bright?

I painted the pathways all silver and white.

I was so fine that night,
*   my benevolent light*
*   shone brighter than day*
so that children might play.

You hadn't a care –
*   and the razor-sharp glare*
of each star
was too far

away
to touch you.

It was all so right, I was full and bright
till the thieves and the witches came,
stealing joy, spinning pain.
Such a shame –
and each gleeful thief
danced barefoot
as he shared out grief.

GARI

I knew Elen was seeing someone. Too bloody right I did. Knew the signs, didn't I? Knew what to look for. Takes one to catch one... and all that. OK, fine, I'm the first to admit I'm no angel. I strayed, I got my share. And that was that. It meant nothing. It was just sex. End of story. Scratched an itch. Filled a gap. Because Elen was... well, she didn't want to know then, did she? But Christ, I never stopped loving her. Even with Liz, I'd close my eyes, so I could come with Elen... so I could love Elen while I ran my fingers through someone else's hair. And I'd never want to stay, not to cuddle Liz afterwards, not to wake up beside her the next morning. Liz was like a fast food fix, best taken standing up: no need to reach for the best china.

When Elen found somebody else, I went cold. Elen with another man, kissing, caressing, sharing, giving. Doing all the things that I wanted to do with her.... I kept quiet. Turned a blind eye. Stuck my head in the sand and gave her some space. What right did I have now to judge her? And when she escaped from the house leaving her excuses behind her, I pretended to be patient, said nothing even though the whole bloody thought of it made me feel sick. Well, it would, wouldn't it? Jesus, every man has his pride. Despite all that, I decided to wait for the phase to pass. It would all blow over, like it did with Liz and me. It was a matter of time before she'd forget about this bloke and come to her senses. Get a grip again. Start wearing longer skirts once more, plainer white knickers with no lace on them.

We slept apart. Her choice. I tried to stay cool about it, but that's when it really started to get to me. The bed felt so big that first night apart. Big and cold. Like an open field. It was as if I had too much room for my legs. And it was awkward and painful to see her things gradually disappear from our room – bits and bobs – bottles of perfume, stuff she used for her hair. But they were her things. Tiny parts of her were slipping away from me and I was helpless, watching her to and fro with feathers for her own private nest just across the landing, shutting the door even more firmly with every 'goodnight' that followed. That was hell. Seeing that door shut. And then thinking of her in there getting undressed, preparing to slip between the fresh sheets to think of him as her small white hands wandered over her body.

One morning I noticed that she'd left her door open. I

74

couldn't resist. Hell, she was still my wife, wasn't she? And I only looked. A quick peek through the door like a schoolboy. She was in her underwear, new stuff probably, because I'd never seen it before. The fuschia-coloured bra lifted her breasts prettily, made her skin look milky white. She wore a matching scrap of something that left nothing to the imagination. And she fancied herself, I could tell, preening in front of the mirror, cupping her breasts in her hands. It began to turn me on. Then I suddenly felt awkward. This wasn't Elen. Guilt came over me as if I were invading the privacy of a complete stranger, of this beautiful, confident woman of whom I knew nothing.

That image remained in my mind. Elen in fuschia-pink underwear and the sun laughing into the spare-room window. Her room, where she kept all her secrets. Then the jealousy began to gnaw at my insides. It came in small bursts at first, like unexpected toothache. Then it worsened, stayed, grew heavy in my gut like a sinister growth and I couldn't bear it any more. I was going to tell her. Ask her. Beg her on my knees if I had to. Elen, please, come back into my life, my bed... our bed.

I chose my evening carefully. A night I knew she'd be home. When she wouldn't have been with him. A nice meal, wine glasses, even candles. I'd swallowed all my pride and Christ, it had a bitter taste to it. But I wanted her, didn't I? Wanted Elen back. She was working late. A parents' evening. I didn't expect to see her until seven at the very least. But it turned eleven and there was no sign of her. The bloody meal was ruined by then and I was pissed off, couldn't understand what had kept her. Any man would conclude she was up to no good. I sat and polished off the wine. The inconsiderate little bitch. And with that bastard, whoever he was! When I heard the back door open at one in the morning I was ready for her. I remember feeling terribly lightheaded. That was the red wine but I was angry too. All worked up. God knows what was going on inside my head, except that I wasn't thinking straight and the need to take my revenge on both of them was tight across my chest. Almost without realising what I was doing I fumbled to unzip my trousers and it felt awkward as if someone else was doing it for me. All I knew was that I had to have her myself. I was going to take her, possess her. Insist on my rights.

I grabbed her arm as she walked in. Her fear was obvious, audible in her throat.

'No, Gari... don't! Don't touch me.... Please... oh, no!'

I thought how pathetic she sounded at the time and that egged me on somehow. The wine was sitting on my brain and I was clumsy, my head fuzzed as if it were full of feathers. I remember the soft tearing sound as her clothes ripped and then I was inside her but she was dry like a piece of apple left out in the sun.

It wasn't pleasure. Or even revenge. Only an instinctive need to prove how much of a man I was. It was a primitive thing. Putting my mark on her in case she strayed again. Elen... sweet Elen. When I got off her I was breathing in spurts, gasping as if I'd been running. She didn't look at me. Not once, during this ugly, enforced coupling. While I took her. She never looked at me. I was the stronger of the two of us. I took possession.... I had my way. The conquering hero. But when it was all over I didn't know how to be. She was trembling. Hunched up. The woman who'd just been raped, holding her blouse together limply, face blank. And then my own cries became louder than everything and I was disgusted with the sounds being ripped from my throat. I was so ashamed now. Of course I .was, God Almighty. Seeing her like that. I began to realise what I'd done and it made me want to vomit. Then the cries inside my throat turned into words, a pathetic flood of words I couldn't hold back.

'Elen... my love... yes, you are my love – that's why... oh, Christ! I never meant to.... It's just because I love you, that's why I....'

It was then that she looked at me. After those words. And I heard my own voice again, humble, desperate, 'I can't blame you now for hating me.'

She moved her head slightly. Lifted her chin. Widened her eyes as though hypnotized. I held my breath as she moved because it was so unexpected. She'd been motionless. Silent. So that it felt as if I'd been breathed on by a statue. And she said, 'I don't hate you.' Then, carefully, calculatingly, she added, as she sensed my desperate, vain hope, 'I don't hate you, Gari. I just love him. More than I ever loved you. More than I ever imagined I could ever love anyone.' Her words were like leaves falling. I wanted to grasp each brittle piece, to crush their fragility. 'I was going to tell you when I got home tonight, but I never got the chance, did I?'

She said it without malice, as if something trivial had prevented her from telling me, like the phone ringing at an inconvenient time. But we both knew what had stopped her. It was an almost visible truth, hanging between us like a mist.

'Tell me what?' But it was obvious. I just said it to fill an empty space.

'That I was having an affair.' Her voice, the words, fell flatly into the void; stones landing in mud.

'Elen, love – d'you think I hadn't guessed, that I didn't know? Look, it doesn't matter. I'll forget about it. We'll put it all behind us – like I did with Liz. We all make mistakes.' I was at it again, pleading with her, begging. And despising my own weakness at the same time.

Elen stood up. Her messed-up hair and ripped stockings gave her a strange dignity, the look of a woman who'd endured great hardship like a war or an earthquake or a flood. It was the look of a survivor.

'I love him,' she said simply. She had dark shadows under her eyes.

'And what about us?'

'There is no – there will never be an "us" again, Gari.'

Cold. So neat and final. And 'never' was a hell of a long time.

'You're going to him, then?' She smiled through her hurt then, but it was just a movement of her face, her mouth mimicking a smile. I pressed her further. Tortured myself. 'Who is he then, Elen? Tell me. Tell me what his name is, at least.'

Her breathing seemed stilted. Her face was the colour of string. I realised with a sudden pang of guilt that she was suffering.

'Owain Wynne,' she said slowly, as if she were reluctant to lose the sound of his name. 'Detective Inspector Owain Wynne. That's what his name was.'

'Was?'

'He died today.'

I froze. And her eyes told me: I've been grieving. Trying to cope. I've been hiding from the rest of the world because the pain and the loss are driving me insane. But it was the words she used which frightened me. Her strength. The fact that her grief was stronger than any feeling she had towards me. Her voice was somehow trapped in her throat, muffled, like a bell wrapped in muslin, 'I had something beautiful – too beautiful, and I was afraid of it slipping away – it was like having a piece of the sun in my hands.'

Then she looked at me. Looked for the past in my face. But I couldn't give it back to her, could I? Couldn't give her yesterday. It reproached me. Little shards of our own days in the sun punctured the images that haunted me.

'It wasn't all a waste of time, was it, Elen? Between us? It didn't used to be like this.'

Her eyes remained still. Filled up. For a moment I imagined she'd turn to me, let me comfort her, hug her.... It was only a moment. I suddenly realised how cold the house had become. The enveloping cold of the early hours.

'I'm going to bed,' she said, almost without moving her lips.

The velvet of her footsteps crept away up the stairs.

And the White Tree spoke from within its mottled branches:

There's a cold breeze thrusting its tongue between my boughs. It quickens, excites, paces its desire as it traces its fingers along the knotted bark. It pouts, it poses, summer-tasting lips of roses... remembering is bittersweet... those games you had of hide-and-seek... two little girls whispering, cheek-to-cheek.

'Come on, Nen,' she'd say. Then you'd follow, so small, so trusting, hair so yellow.

She was in charge as autumn ran red through her tresses. You lay down and let her cover you with leaves, your legs, your arms, your little white neck, your face, your hair.

'No, Medi, don't!'

And hearing her name was no surprise. I'd known it forever. September itself, a long brown name like bracken and berries.

You wept. Every tear meant:
    'I don't like it here.'

Beneath the leaves. Autumn's coverlet. Your eyelashes wet...
Let me out...

Come along, darling Nen – come here to me: let the old woman of Coed Esyllt embrace you as she bares her barren breasts....

You climbed then without fear, higher and higher until your thighs ached;

you saw summer's bier
from up here –
all so clear.

Now you were the strong one,
way up high,
no longer shy.

She could not reach you.
Could she, Nen?
Then you threw back your head,
laughed aloud,
saw eyes, nose, a mouth

within a startled cloud:

'Look up, Medi! Look! It's God's face!'

God is Love.
As she stood there and coveted what she saw from above.

MEDI

He stood there on my doorstep, the day damp upon his hair. He looked at me. His eyes seemed dangerously vacant.

'Is she here?' He didn't say your name.

'No.'

And then he laughed loudly. A raucous, open-mouthed laugh, baring his teeth.

'I don't know what she sees in you,' he said. There was a malicious ring to his voice as he almost chanted the words like a wilful child. 'Bloody lesbian!'

He was watching me too carefully, willing me to rise to the bait. And my heart bled, Nen. Because of what he was. Because of the years you had wasted on him. Because of his venom. I began to shut the door. What followed was

85

like a scene in a lousy film. A film whose trashy soundtrack disguised an even trashier script and a predictable bad guy with his foot wedged in the door. But this was my door being used without permission. And the bad guy said: 'I know full well what you get up to. Don't think for a minute that I don't! Oh, people will get to hear of this, don't you worry. The courts – because I'll be naming you. You do understand that, don't you? And the papers. They'll lap it up. Be a scoop, won't it? A man's wife has an affair – with a woman! Christ! A right bloody freak show!'

Cut.

Yes, it was an award-winning performance. Plenty of poison. Hate. Convincing words. But the bad guy had a blob of spit on his chin. That wasn't in the script. And now he was rewriting that too, misconstruing everything for his own ends....

Cut.

Foot removed from door.

But there would be no re-take. No second chance. No cutting-edge director in a leather jacket to run his fingers through his hair and swear profusely. No-one in charge. Only lousy actors ad-libbing for all they were worth, shit timing and dodgy lighting.

I wasn't your lover, was I, Nen? And he knew that: he wasn't even kidding himself. Maybe it would have been easier in the long run for Gari to stomach that – you and me. Maybe another woman wouldn't have threatened his masculinity in quite the same way. If we'd been lovers, that is. Eventually he'd have managed to convince himself that our affair had been no more than a special bond between lifelong friends. His see-black or see-white, no-grey-bits kind of logic would have helped him cope, convinced him he could win you back and the structure of his humdrum life would be safe again – ironed shirts, shiny floors, house, garden, car, you....

That is, if we'd been lovers. But we weren't. Were we, Nen? That's not the way you were made.

I remember deciding then that I wasn't going to look at him, at his face, at the white malice forming a crust at the corners of his mouth. And then, suddenly, it all went quiet. Nothing. He wasn't there in front of me any more. He was nothing but fading footsteps – soft sounds on a hard surface, like a wet towel dripping into a bath.

This was before he knew about Owain. When he started suspecting you, following you. Before you admitted everything to him. Before the police cross-examined him. They'd kept him in overnight – just long enough to send him near the edge, to stir up his feelings, arouse other people's suspicions. They always suspect husbands first, don't they, when wives disappear into thin air, walk out of their own lives. And Gari was the perfect suspect this time, wasn't he, Nen? The unreasonable husband. The one who'd been hurt. The one whose pretty, blonde wife had been cheating on him. Even that hadn't been enough for her, had it? She preferred her lover's ghost to her husband of flesh and blood. That was the worst thing, the last straw – her love affair with a memory. Isn't that the truth, Mr Rees? You were mad at her, weren't you? Angry and hurt. Of course you were. Wouldn't any husband in your situation have felt exactly the same? Angry. Bitter. Desperate. That's understandable. What did you do with the body, Mr Rees?

I never... no... I didn't... I've no idea who....

Then he cried a little. Got worked up. He was sincere. That's a terrible thing. Cruel. When you're telling the whole truth, nothing but the truth and nobody'll believe you. Yes, he cried, his ashen cheeks soaking up his tears like blotting paper. Grey on grey like rain on a dirty window. I didn't do it. I didn't kill her. And he was forced to imagine how that would have felt, Nen – how it would have felt to put his hands around your white neck and squeeze, press down – hard, so hard, harder than he'd ever thought it would be... that slender neck so deceptively strong, like a swan's, fighting back; beauty with a sting in its tail.

What did you do, Mr Rees? Follow her? You knew her as well as anybody did. Where would she go? Who would she turn to? Where? Where would she go when she needed to escape? When she wanted space? The mountain paths? Down by the sea? Or to Coed Esyllt, the woods where she played as a child, where the leaves smelt of their own fragrant decay and overripe nuts would crack underfoot? Is that where she went? And then... what then? No, of course not. You don't remember what happened then. Or are you refusing to remember? Refusing to think of yourself digging under the dead leaves where the insects were, where the soft crumbs of earth got under your fingernails like a macabre dough mix. Is that what happened? Digging, burying?

He denied it. God Almighty, no! That's not what

happened. I don't know what happened to her! And the silent scream inside him seemed to want to explode. Because that was how it was. Because he knew nothing. But they didn't know that, did they? They were just doing their duty. Searching for the truth. Searching for you.

Nobody knows, do they, Nen? Nobody saw. You arrived in the dark. You'd got your feet wet. I took off your soft shoes and put them out to dry in front of the fire. Pretty lace patterns began to form in their dampness. I caressed your cold toes, massaged the warmth of my hands into them. You didn't pull away as you usually did as you couldn't bear your feet to be touched! But you weren't ticklish that night; you were numb. Didn't pull away.

Your hair, your long blonde hair, was soaked too, tamed by the damp that had possessed you and made you shiver like a frightened rabbit. You used to love it years ago when I played with your hair, brushing, combing, plaiting. And that's what I did that night. Brushed, combed, plaited. Right hand, left hand, over, under until I had a golden chain to wind around your bare neck. It suited you, Nen. A decoration. Virgin gold blushing in the fire's glow.

You looked so pretty. Just like a child pretending to be asleep. Pretty pretend-sleep as your lips tried to resist a smile. Like old times – pretending to sleep as the leaves tickled your nostrils and made you want to sneeze! Playing at sleeping, at hiding-and-seeking under the White Tree.

But this wasn't make-believe, was it, Nen? Wasn't child's play.

Your forehead was warm for a long time, your lips warm on my lips... *sleep, dear child, within my arms...* the

89

fire's heat brought a glow to your cheeks, caressed you...
flame by dancing flame... *you will never come to harm*....

You needed to sleep.

Like I needed to pretend that you loved me.

And a husky-voiced September said:

It's getting colder; the days are shorter. Mine are the long nights wrapping their black-cats' tails around the branches.

To myself I am true
while I watch the awakening dark,
and now I have you.

Forgive me: I can't offer you the warmth of the sun. I have only the leaves and their quick rustling which is like the turning of pages. They are your coverlet once more, teasing you, concealing you as you lie at the foot of the shadowy oak where the earth is starry with dew –

but I can hide you, Nen.

Hide-and-seek again.

It's a game like before where you have to trust me

while God himself hides his face

in the White Tree.